This book belongs to

_____

Crazy for Hockey!

Five All-Star Stories

Crazy for Hockey!

Five All-Star Stories

GILLES TIBO

ILLUSTRATIONS BY
BRUNO ST-AUBIN

Scholastic Canada Ltd.
Toronto New York London Auckland Sydney
Mexico City New Delhi Hong Kong Buenos Aires

Scholastic Canada Ltd.
604 King Street West, Toronto, Ontario M5V 1E1, Canada

Scholastic Inc.
557 Broadway, New York, NY 10012, USA

Scholastic Australia Pty Limited
PO Box 579, Gosford, NSW 2250, Australia

Scholastic New Zealand Limited
Private Bag 94407, Botany, Manukau 2163, New Zealand

Scholastic Children's Books
Euston House, 24 Eversholt Street, London NW1 1DB, UK

www.scholastic.ca

Library and Archives Canada Cataloguing in Publication
Tibo, Gilles, 1951-
[Works. Selections. English]
Crazy for hockey! : five all-star stories / Gilles Tibo ; illustrated
by Bruno St-Aubin ; translated by Petra Johannson.
Translation of: Nicolas fou de hockey!
ISBN 978-1-4431-0744-0 (hardcover)
I. St-Aubin, Bruno, illustrator II. Johannson, Petra, translator
III. Title.
PS8589.I26A2 2017   jC843'.54   C2017-901767-5

7 6 5 4 3 2   Printed in Malaysia 108   18 19 20 21 22

TABLE OF CONTENTS

To all the hockey fanatics.
— Gilles Tibo and Bruno St-Aubin

Where's My Hockey Sweater?

It was Saturday. Nicholas snuggled happily under the covers, dreaming of the day ahead. This morning was the first hockey practice of the season.

UH OH! Suddenly he remembered. He had to find his equipment. Quick as a flash, he jumped out of bed, tripped over his stuff, and fell flat on his face.

5

Where was his championship hockey sweater? Nicholas started searching. All he could find were shirts and socks and pyjamas. YAY! There were his shoulder pads.

Then he looked for his helmet. He found
a tuque, a baseball cap and a wizard's hat.
YAY! There were his shin guards.

Still no hockey sweater. No helmet either. And where were his skates? Nicholas found rain boots and ski boots and flip-flops. YAY! There were his hockey pants.

He hunted all over his bedroom, but he just couldn't find the rest of his equipment.

Nicholas crawled out over his mess.

His mom and dad were in the kitchen.

"You're only half dressed!" said his dad. "Hockey practice starts in an hour!"

"But I can't find my sweater or my helmet or my skates."

"I think I saw your skates in the garage," said his mom. "You've got to keep track of your stuff."

Nicholas headed for the garage. He
checked the cupboards and the shelves.
He searched through all the boxes.
Finally, he found his skates.

Nicholas rushed back to the kitchen and gulped down some cereal. He still had to find his sweater and his helmet. And his hockey stick!

"I think I saw your helmet in the basement," said his dad. "You've got to keep track of your stuff."

Nicholas raced down to the basement. He rummaged under the workbench and behind the suitcases and through the toy boxes. Finally, he found his helmet.

Nicholas ran back to the kitchen and gobbled some toast with peanut butter. Now to find his hockey stick and his sweater.

"I think I saw your hockey stick under the porch," said his sister. "You've got to keep track of your stuff, Nicholas."

There was no time to lose. He ran outside
and looked under the porch. He found pails and
shovels and dump trucks, and finally, his hockey
stick!

Nicholas hurried back to the kitchen and grabbed a blueberry muffin. Now he just needed to find his sweater.

"Didn't I see your sweater in your bedroom?"
his mom asked. "You know, Nicholas, you've got
to keep track of your stuff."

Nicholas ran back to his room. What a MESS!
He would never be able to find his sweater in there.

He pulled them on as fast as he could and looked in the mirror. "I'm ready to go!" he called.

"Congratulations!" cried his mom.
"You look like a real pro," said his dad.
Nicholas looked at the clock. "We have
to go! The practice starts in 15 minutes!"

29

"Wait a second," said his mom.
"I'm not sure where I put my car keys . . ."

31

Nicholas was happily reading in bed when his dad barged into the room.

"Guess what, son? The goalie on your team is sick. How do you feel about playing in net tomorrow?"

"Sure!" said Nicholas, without thinking. "No problem!"

His dad tucked him in and kissed him goodnight.
Nicholas lay in the dark, his eyes wide open. He
kept thinking, *I . . . I . . . I've never stopped a puck in
my life!*

Nicholas couldn't get to sleep. To get his mind off the game, he looked out the window. The moon was like a giant hockey puck. The clouds were like huge nets. The stars were champion shooters — and they were about to score on his net! Nicholas lay awake, wishing tomorrow would never come.

Seconds, minutes and hours ticked by.
Nicholas couldn't sleep a wink. When
morning came, he was completely exhausted.

His dad rushed in. "Hurry, Nicholas! The coach dropped off the equipment. The team is waiting for you at the rink!"

Nicholas got out of bed. His eyes were barely open. He skidded on a racing car. BAM! He crashed to the floor.

40

Half asleep, he headed for the
kitchen. WHAM! He walked
into the door frame.

He sat down at the table. SPLOOSH!
Face-first into the cereal bowl.

He tried to brush his teeth. ZZZZZ . . .
He fell asleep against the mirror.

While Nicholas dozed, his family
tried to get him into the goalie gear.
It wasn't easy because he was so
floppy. All he was dreaming
about was sleep, sleep
and more sleep!

45

At last Nicholas was all geared up. He managed to stuff himself into the car, goalie pads and all.

His dad looked at his watch. "We're going to be late!" he said.

He stepped on the gas. VROOM!
Nicholas snoozed, dreaming that
he was back in bed.

SCREECH! The car came to a halt outside the arena. Nicholas bolted awake. His dad checked his watch again. "Come on, Nicholas! The game starts in three minutes!"

They hurried through the doors into the arena. Nicholas's heart stopped. The stands were packed. His team was warming up on the ice. The coach rushed over. "Okay, Nicholas! Go get in net!"

His dad gave him a wink and a tap on the helmet. "Go on, Nicholas! You're the best!"

Nicholas headed for the net. His heart was pounding. He took a look at the opposing players. They seemed huge — and mean. It was like a bad dream.

The game began. Nicholas could barely keep his eyes open. All through the first period, he yawned and stretched — and stopped the puck. The crowd cheered.

He dropped to his knees to rest a little
— and made more saves. The crowd
cheered and bounced in their seats.

In the second period, Nicholas was even sleepier. He leaned on one goalpost, then the other — and stopped more pucks. The crowd cheered, bounced in their seats and threw their arms in the air!

In the third period, Nicholas was so drowsy that he dropped to the ice for a nap. He stopped even *more* pucks! The crowd cheered, bounced in their seats and threw their arms in the air, chanting NI-CHO-LAS! NI-CHO-LAS! NI-CHO-LAS! while they did the wave.

57

At last the game was over. Nicholas's team had won 6–0! There was a standing ovation. Nicholas's teammates rushed over to congratulate him and carry him on their shoulders. But he was too groggy to smile.

In the change room, the coach told Nicholas's
dad, "Your son is amazing. He's a natural goalie.
He anticipates the shots! He's so laid-back!
What cool! What leadership!"

"Um, yes, he amazed us all," said his dad proudly.

60

But Nicholas didn't hear any more.
He was fast asleep — at last!

Nicholas was lying in bed, dreaming that he was on a warm tropical beach.

Suddenly, his dad barged into the room, yelling, "Hurry! Hurry, Nicholas! Wake up!"

His mom rushed into the room next,
shouting, "Nicholas! I made your lunch!"

Then his sister ran in and jumped on his bed, saying, "Nicholas! I made you a good luck charm!"

His dad started giving him advice before
Nicholas was even out of bed. "Dress warmly,
Nicholas. Arenas are often chilly."
"Yeah, yeah, Dad . . ." he answered sleepily.

At breakfast, his mother said, "Eat up,
Nicholas! You need your energy. You're facing
the best team in the league today!"
"Yeah, yeah, Mom!" he replied.

While he was brushing his teeth, his dad kept on. "Don't forget, Nicholas, you need to keep the ice in front of your net clean. Concentrate, cover your corners and remember your peripheral vision!"

Before leaving the house, his mother handed him
a water bottle, his lunch box and more advice.

"Nicholas, don't forget to eat and stay hydrated.
Make sure your skates are tight and that your
helmet is done up properly. Remember your
shoulder and knee pads, too!"

"Yeah, yeah, Mom!" said Nicholas.

On the way, Nicholas's father told him about
all the best NHL games. He described every single
winning goal in every single Stanley Cup final.
He explained the famous Canada–Russia hockey
series to him in great detail. Nicholas's head was
OVERFLOWING with hockey.

At the arena, Nicholas slipped into the players'
dressing room. While they got ready, the coach
told the team all about their opponents:

"Number 16 — a real bully!

"Number 22 — he can't turn right.

"Number 64 — likes to elbow.

"Number 44 — careful, he's a scrapper!"

The team was so scared that every player
was frozen in place.

Coach showed everyone the game plan.
He drew the players and explained all
the plays the team should make.

Ten minutes later, the board was filled with pictures and arrows, dotted lines and directions. Nicholas and his teammates didn't understand a thing. Suddenly, his stomach hurt. His throat was tight. His head ached.

Their heads filled with lines, arrows, stick men and plays, Nicholas and his team hopped on the ice. The arena was overflowing and the crowd was wild. As Nicholas skated toward the net, all he could hear was people yelling.

Go, Matthew!

Hurry, hurry, Paolo!

As he neared the net, Nicholas heard his dad call out, "Come on, Nicholas! You're the best!"

The referee dropped the puck
and the game began.

Moms and dads, brothers and sisters, aunts
and uncles, grandfathers and grandmothers
shouted out advice:

"Faster, Sebastian, faster! Score!"

"Max! Keep the puck! Keep the puck!"

"Hurry, Luigi! Pass the puck! Pass it!"

"Paolo, what are you doing?"

79

It was impossible for the players to concentrate. Both teams were playing worse and worse. Nicholas's defensemen were like sieves, letting every puck through.

Behind him, Nicholas heard his dad yelling: "Be careful, Nicholas. On your right! No, your left! Raise your stick! No, go down low! No, no, no! Stand up! Watch out in front of you! No, behind the net!"

Nicholas was so overwhelmed by all the advice, he couldn't concentrate. By the end of the first period, the other team was ahead by five goals. What a disaster!

Between periods, the players rushed to their dressing room. The coach was furious! He drew another game plan but none of the players understood a single thing.

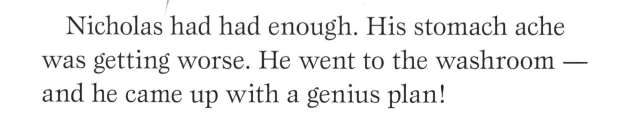

Nicholas had had enough. His stomach ache
was getting worse. He went to the washroom —
and he came up with a genius plan!

84

Nicholas hopped back onto the ice. While the crowd shouted, while the coaches yelled, while the players got more and more worked up, Nicholas was calm. Nicholas was cool. Nicholas was serene.

His defensemen were still letting shot after shot get past them, but Nicholas's concentration was unbreakable. He stopped every single puck. No one could score on him.

Between the second and third periods, Nicholas shared his master plan with his teammates. One by one, each team member went into the washroom and walked back out wearing a huge smile on his face.

In the third period, despite all the noise, despite all the yelling, despite all the mayhem, Nicholas's team was calm. Nicholas's team was cool. Nicholas's team was serene. They passed the puck with such precision, they scored TEN goals.

Bam!

Boom!

Bing!

At last the game was over. Nicholas's team
had won 10–5! All the players were smiling.

Pictures were taken, video was shot,
but when asked about the game, no one
on the team answered.

90

More and more questions were asked,
but still none of the players replied.

That's when Nicholas and all his teammates reached up and removed their ear plugs!

A Very Hockey Christmas

It was only four days until Christmas! Nicholas was spinning round and round the Christmas tree, trying to sneak a peek at all the presents underneath.

"Nicholas, you're giving me a headache!" said his father.

"You're making me dizzy," his mother sighed.

"And you're getting on my last nerve!" his sister added.

Three days before Christmas, Nicholas tried a more subtle approach. He bent down and pretended to tie his shoelaces, then picked up a present and gave it a shake. He said he was looking for the cat behind the Christmas tree and poked at a few more gifts.

He even did somersaults in the living room, and not-so-accidentally bumped into a box or two.

"Nicholas, if you keep this up, you won't get any presents this year," grumbled his father.

Two days before Christmas, Nicholas couldn't stand it anymore. The wait was driving him crazy! He checked his Christmas list one more time.

Dear Santa,

Please send:

  Hockey jersey
  Hockey gloves
  Hockey socks
  Hockey pads
  Hockey skates
  Hockey books

Well, anything hockey, really!

Finally, after counting down the days, the hours, the minutes and the seconds, it was Christmas Eve! Nicholas's parents had cooked a holiday feast to feed twenty. But there were only four people in Nicholas's family. What was going on? Were Santa and his elves coming for dinner?

Suddenly, ding-dong! The doorbell rang. But it wasn't Santa Claus.

"Ho, ho, ho! Merry Christmas!" cried Nicholas's grandparents, uncles, aunts and cousins, as they all streamed into the house.

More presents were placed under the tree. Some of them were even for Nicholas! But he was not allowed to open them until Christmas morning.

After a huge dinner, everyone got ready for bed. The whole family was sleeping over. Nicholas, his sister and their cousins were staying in the basement. They played hide-and-seek. They had pillow fights. Finally, they crawled into their sleeping bags and fell fast asleep.

On Christmas morning, Grandma woke everyone. "Come quick!" she said. "Santa's been here!"

They raced upstairs and piled into the living
room. There were presents EVERYWHERE!
Nicholas's father started handing them out.
His sister got the book she wanted. His cousins
whooped with joy as they unwrapped their
presents! And Nicholas got the best gift of all . . .
a hockey helmet!

But the helmet was much too big. Nicholas's head was swimming inside it.

While his sister and cousins tore the wrapping off more gifts, Nicholas opened another: shoulder pads. Enormous shoulder pads.

Next came a hockey jersey — a hockey jersey for a giant! Then came socks that were far too long.

In the next box were the biggest shin pads
Nicholas had ever seen.

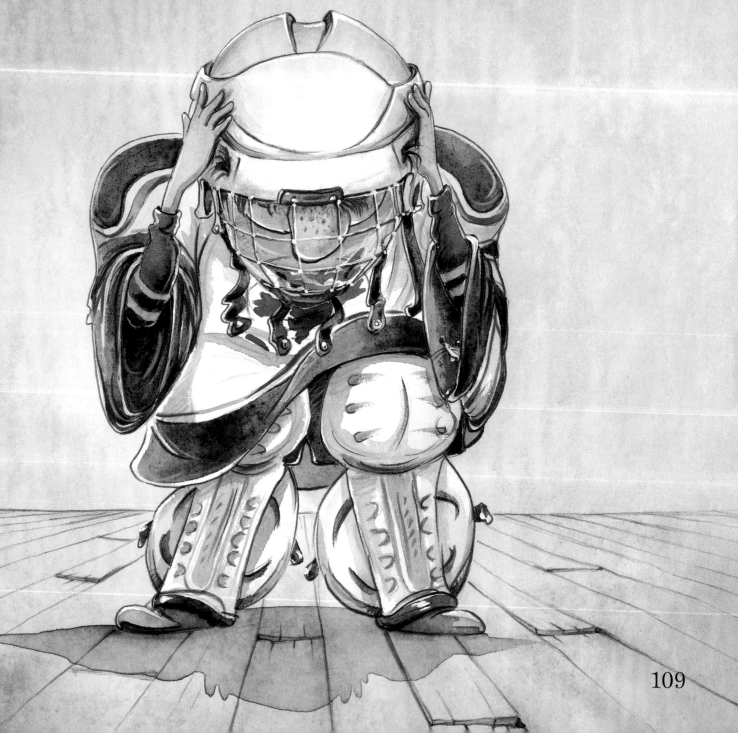

Finally, it was time to open Santa's present: hockey skates! But just like everything else, the skates were much too big.

"Don't worry, Nicholas," his mother reassured him. "Feet are what grow the fastest!"

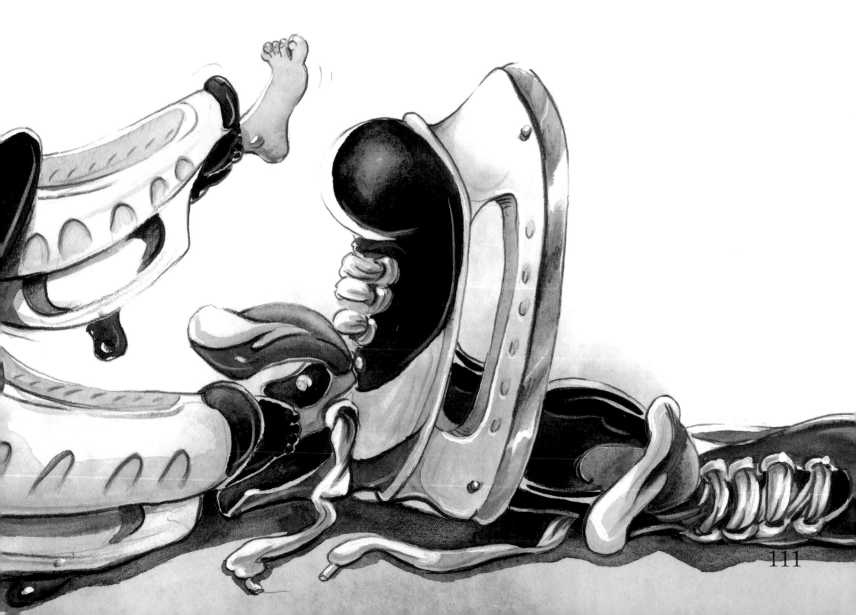

While his cousins ran off to play with their fantastic new stuff, Nicholas sat alone, surrounded by all his too-big, too-large, too-long hockey equipment.

Even though he wasn't feeling very cheerful, Nicholas decided to call his friends and wish them a Merry Christmas. To his surprise, he found out that his friends all had the same problem. Everyone else had received hockey gear, too. Hockey gear that was too big or too small, too wide or too tight.

Nicholas watched the snow falling outside.
Suddenly, he had an idea!

He called back his friends and they all agreed.
It was a fabulous plan!

Nicholas hung up the phone and told his
family that he was going outside to show all
his new hockey equipment to his friends.

"Great idea!" said his grandfather.

Nicholas threw all his gifts into a bag and ran outside.

His friends were already there, each with a bag of his own.

They dumped out their bags on the sidewalk.
All the little players traded their gear with the
bigger ones. Soon everyone had new equipment
that fit perfectly!

Nicholas went back inside wearing hockey gear that was just right.

The whole family admired him.

"Wow! Nicholas! You look great!"

"Just like a real pro!"

"Everything is perfect!"

"Thank you, thank you, thank you!" said Nicholas. He kissed his parents, his grandparents, his uncles and aunts, and told them it was the best Christmas ever!

Everyone smiled back at him except his mother, who was staring down at him with a puzzled look . . .

121

. . . wondering how Nicholas had grown up so fast!

Nicholas was on his way to school when he met his new neighbour.

"Hi, my name's Jeremy," said the boy. "We just moved in."

"I'm Nicholas. Welcome to the neighbourhood!"

They walked to school together, talking all the way. After the first block, they had covered robots. By the end of the second block, they'd talked about biking. And on the third block, it was all about comics.

125

When they got to the schoolyard,
Nicholas introduced his new friend.
"Hey, everyone. This is Jeremy!"
"Hi, Jeremy!"
"Welcome!"
"Hello!"

They joined the soccer game but it quickly became clear that Jeremy was not a good player. Big Dan stopped playing and rolled his eyes. Soon everyone else was following his lead, as usual.

The bell rang and everyone headed in. Jeremy followed Nicholas and chose the seat next to him. The teacher asked the class to give Jeremy a warm welcome. Everyone applauded politely but they were all looking at Dan. He was rolling his eyes even more.

That evening, Nicholas headed to the park with his friends to play soccer.

"Can I play with you guys?" Jeremy called out.

Nicholas answered, "Sure!" But nobody else even stopped.

They got to the park and started kicking
the ball around. Jeremy couldn't keep up,
and soon nobody would pass him the ball.

Jeremy's troubles continued when he came out to play baseball at the park. When teams were chosen, he was the last to be picked. He spent most of his time on the bench watching everyone else play, not saying a word.

It was the same with every sport. In basketball, he was able to get by the big players but he couldn't get the ball in the basket.

At judo, he was quick to hide between
the legs of his opponents.

Every time Nicholas came to Jeremy's
defence, everyone said, "What? Can't
Jeremy stand up for himself?"

One morning on the way to school, Nicholas saw Jeremy sitting on his front steps. When he joined him, he could see that Jeremy's eyes were filled with tears.

Jeremy stared down at the ground. He told
Nicholas what it had been like in his old town.
"I didn't have many friends," he said. "And
it's happening all over again."

137

"Well, what do you like to do best?"
Nicholas asked him.

Wiping away a tear, Jeremy answered,
"I love skating and I'd love to play hockey,
but I don't think I would be very good."

"But you're so fast!" said Nicholas. "You have all the qualities of a great scorer. All you need is some training."

"But I don't have a coach!" replied Jeremy.

"*I* know a good coach!" Nicholas smiled. "Me!"

Nicholas spent that whole school day coming up with a training plan. That night after dinner, he went over to Jeremy's with hockey sticks and balls.

The training began . . . in secret! Nicholas taught Jeremy how to control the ball, how to deke around an opponent and how to score a goal.

As the days and weeks passed, Jeremy's skills improved. He was playing like a real champion. Nicholas had to work harder and harder to block his shots.

As soon as it was cold enough outside, Nicholas asked his dad to make a backyard rink. Jeremy came over to practise. It turned out he was a great skater! Nicholas lent him his old hockey equipment. It was too big, but Jeremy didn't mind.

Together, they practised, practised and practised until they were worn out. Jeremy had become such a strong skater and shooter that Nicholas couldn't stop him.

One night, Nicholas's dad called Jeremy's dad, who called Nicholas's coach. The coach said that Jeremy could try out for the team at the next practice.

The big day arrived. Jeremy and Nicholas went to the arena together.

When they walked into the dressing room, everyone rolled their eyes at Jeremy. No one said a word to him.

Jeremy and Nicholas gritted their teeth and dressed for practice. Nicholas couldn't believe how his friends were acting.

When they got on the ice, the coach split the players into two teams, and Nicholas skated to his net. Jeremy and Nicholas were on opposite sides! When Jeremy realized he was on the same team as Dan, he got so nervous that he lost his balance and fell on the ice. Everyone laughed.

Jeremy looked over at Nicholas.
Then, red as a tomato, he got up and
joined the rest of his team.

The coach blew the whistle to start the game. The first chance he got, Jeremy went for the puck, wove through the defencemen, passed the puck through their legs, spun around, skated forward, then backwards, then spun around again and . . . found himself in front of the net!

Nicholas was so surprised that he didn't have a chance to stop the puck. Jeremy shot and SCORED! His whole team cheered, even Dan.

Jeremy scored two goals each period for a grand total of six goals! He was the highest scorer of the game!

At the final whistle, everyone rushed over and congratulated him. The celebration continued into the dressing room, where Big Dan lifted Jeremy up in the air. He was the hero of the day!

As for Nicholas . . .

. . . he had never been so happy to lose a hockey game!